Little Bears go Shopping

Heather Maisner

Illustrated by
Tomislav Zlatic

W
FRANKLIN WATTS
LONDON•SYDNEY

Evie

Jack

Lily

Harry

Hello. I'm Big Bear. Today I'm going shopping with the little bears. And I've brought my shopping bag and shopping list with me.

Olivia

But the little bears keep knocking things over, running away and losing their belongings. Can you help me, please?

Vase

Knitting wool

Brush

Here we are at the household shop. The little bears have caused chaos. Can you point to where these things belong?

Grater

Bread bin

Pepper grinder

Rubbish bin

Thank you. But did you hear a noise? I think Jack Bear is hiding here. Can you see him?

And can you see the blue wallet Jack was holding?

Trousers

Dress

Now we are in the clothes shop. The little bears have been trying on T-shirts, dresses and trousers. They've also dropped lots of things on the floor. But where do they belong?

Red sock

Underpants

Yellow
T-shirt

Skirt

Thank you. I think little Evie Bear is hiding here. Can you see her?

And she's lost her hair bow.
Can you find it, please?

Birthday card

Felt-tip pens

Sketch pad

Here we are in the book shop. The little bears have moved far too many things around and they've dropped a lot, too. Can you put these things back on the shelves, please?

Picture book

Wrapping paper

Box file

Did you hear that sound? Lily Bear just called out. Can you see her?

Can you find the green
bag she was holding?

The electrical shop is very confusing. The little bears have looked at all sorts of things, and they've moved them all about. Please help me put them back.

Torch

Mobile phone

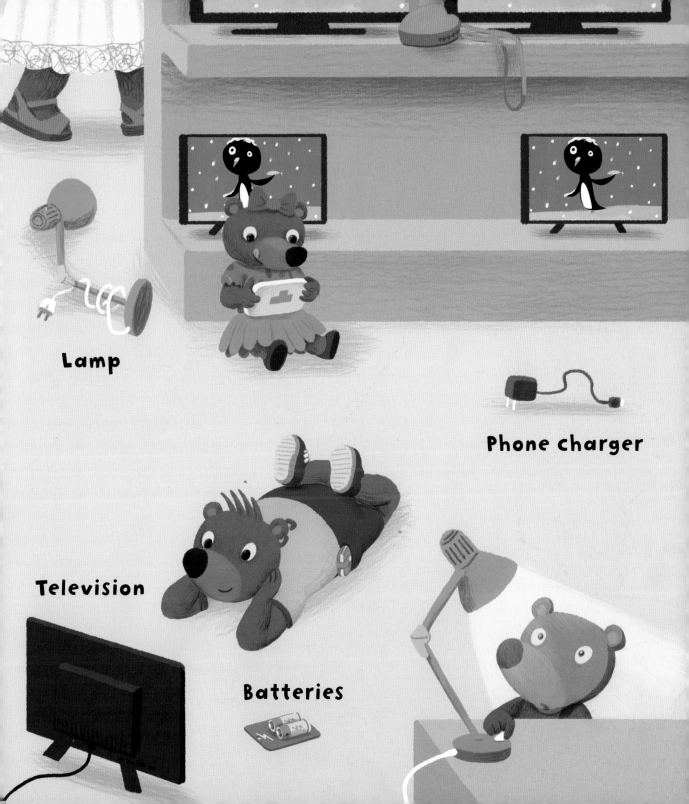

Lamp

Phone charger

Television

Batteries

Thank you so much. Now can you please find Olivia Bear.

And look out for her pink handbag.

She seems to have left it somewhere.

The little bears love toys and sports. Just look at all the things they've played with! Can you put them back, please?

Rugby ball

Cuddly monkey

Badminton net

Tennis racket

Doll

Box of
building bricks

Thank you. Now please find Harry Bear and the red money belt he was wearing.

Time to go home at last, and now we must wait
for the bus. I've put a coloured label on each
little bear's ticket. Can you give them the right
tickets to match their clothes?

And hand them each their
own carrier bag, please.

Thank you. But where did I put my
brown wallet? Can you find it, please?

Everything has been put away and all the bears are busy reading.
Thank you so much. I do hope you'll call by again.

More from the Little Bears!

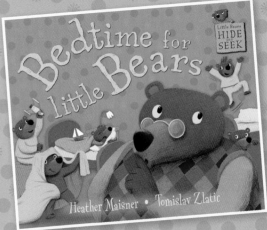

978 1 4451 4323 1

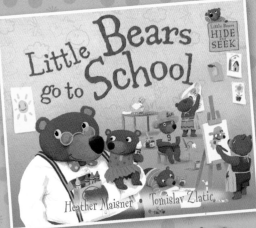

978 1 4451 4327 9

978 1 4451 4329 3

Franklin Watts
Published in paperback in Great Britain in 2019
by The Watts Publishing Group

Text copyright © Heather Maisner 2016
Illustrations © Tomislav Zlatic 2016

Series Editor: Sarah Peutrill
Cover Designer: Cathryn Gilbert
ISBN: 978 1 4451 4325 5

Printed in China

Franklin Watts
An imprint of
Hachette Children's Group
Part of The Watts Publishing Group
Carmelite House
50 Victoria Embankment
London EC4Y 0DZ

An Hachette UK Company
www.hachette.co.uk

www.franklinwatts.co.uk